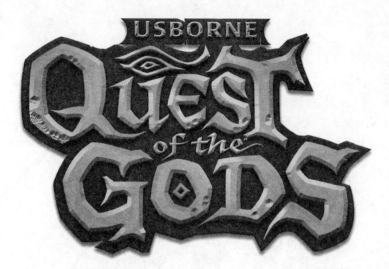

# LAIR OF THE
# WINGED MONSTER

## DAN HUNTER

# THE PROPHECY OF THE SPHINX

THE SPHINX AM I
GUARDIAN OF THE PYRAMIDS
KEEPER OF SECRETS

THE PAST I REMEMBER
THE PRESENT I SEE
THE FUTURE I FORETELL

WHEN THE PHARAOH SHALL DIE
AT THE HANDS OF HIS SON
A PLAGUE SHALL FALL UPON EGYPT

THE LORD OF STORMS WILL RISE AGAIN
THE GOOD GODS WILL BE CHAINED
AND MONSTERS WILL WALK THE LAND

THE SACRED RIVER SHALL SLOW AND DRY
THE SUN WILL SCORCH THE LAND LIKE FIRE
THE STREETS OF EGYPT SHALL RUN WITH BLOOD

BUT HOPE WILL COME FROM THE SOUTH
A HERO OF THE WHEATFIELDS
A KING WITHOUT A KINGDOM

THE LAST OF HIS FAMILY
A LOST CHILD OF HORUS
HE SHALL BATTLE THE MONSTERS TO FREE THE GODS

HE WILL CLAIM THE WHITE CROWN
HE WILL CLAIM THE RED CROWN
HE WILL RULE ALL EGYPT

THE SPHINX AM I
THESE SECRETS I SHARE
GUARD THEM WELL

# MANU'S MAP OF ANCIENT EGYPT

*NILE DELTA*

Heliopolis

Giza

Saqqara

*RED SEA*

Temple of Set

*EASTERN DESERT*

Nubt

*HIGH DESERT*

Waset and Karnak

Entrance to the
Underworld

Temple of Horus

Nebyt

*THE NILE*

N

Fortress of Fire

*SAHARA DESERT*

S

# PROLOGUE

*The soldiers had been standing in lines under the boiling Egyptian sun for an hour already, but not one of them moved or uttered a word of complaint. A lucky few were in the shadow cast by the high palace walls. The rest could do nothing but stand and sweat, waiting for the royal inspection to begin.*

*The brand new shields they carried felt as heavy as rocks, but they could easily have borne the heat and the exhaustion for many more hours. Every one of them knew there were a lot worse things that could happen. They only had to look up at the walls to be reminded of that. The bodies of those who had displeased Pharaoh Oba hung there.*

7

*And above the bodies hovered a cloud of vultures that were not going hungry these days.*

*A sudden blare of trumpets sent the vultures flapping up in surprise. The young Pharaoh Oba strode into the courtyard, wearing the Double Crown of Egypt and a dazzling white robe.*

*Every single soldier thumped his chest in salute. A deafening shout went up: "Long life to the Pharaoh! Victory to the Chosen One of Set!"*

*Oba began to walk up and down the ranks, scowling into faces. Wherever he looked, soldiers stiffened in fear and stared straight ahead.*

*These were brutal men, with scars and reputations as ruthless fighters. Each one had killed dozens. In the inns and the streets, people would hurry out of their way. But this* sour-faced boy terrified them more than a pit full of cobras, even though he was not yet old enough to grow a beard. One glance from those cruel eyes, one snap of his fingers, and it could be them hanging up there on the walls.

Behind Oba followed Bukhu, the High Priest, ever patient, ever ready to smooth over his Pharaoh's angry tantrums. He waited until Oba gave him a nod to show he was satisfied, then he unrolled a scroll and began to read.

"Honoured ones! You are the Pharaoh's own warrior elite, his hand-picked Fangs of Set!" Bukhu gestured to the red-painted symbol on their shields, the jackal-like emblem of Set, God of Darkness. "Be glad! Be proud! Know that the Pharaoh values you above all others!"

Oba gave a hideous grin.

"Because you are the best of the best," Bukhu went on, "you have been chosen to carry out a very important mission. A mission that must not fail!"

The soldiers glanced at one another. They were all thinking the same thing: failure was death. Up on the walls, two vultures fought noisily over a grisly morsel.

"Your beloved Pharaoh," said Bukhu, "is facing a sinister threat from a pretender to his crown. Learn the traitor's name now, all of you, so you may cut it out of his heart: Akori. Say it."

"Akori," went the mumble through the ranks. The boy Pharaoh scowled, as if someone had tipped vinegar down his throat.

Bukhu boomed, "You all remember how our friend and ally, the mighty Set, defeated the upstart God Horus and cast four more of the so-called 'good Gods' into magical prisons?"

The soldiers nodded instantly.

"That should have begun a new era of glory and conquest! Egypt should have risen to become ruler of the world! Instead, my friends, we have been undermined. By means of foul magic, treachery and cheap tricks, Akori has freed three of the rebel Gods."

Nobody said a word, but amazement showed on all of their faces. How could one boy do all of that?

"But his rebellion will not stop there, oh no. He seeks to free them all!" Bukhu, normally so calm, was nearly screaming now. "He will stop at nothing!" He pointed a shaking finger at Oba. "He intends to free Horus, and lead a rebellion against the rightful Pharaoh!"

"Death to the traitor!" yelled a warrior in the front rank.

A sudden silence fell across the courtyard. All the soldiers held their breath. Then Oba smiled broadly and clapped his hands, and all the other warriors began to shout "Death to the traitor!" too. Baying like wolves, they called for Akori's blood as they stamped their feet on the ground. They had forgotten all about their fear. They hammered on their shields with their sword hilts until Bukhu held up his hands for silence.

"The Fangs of Set shall have the honour of ending this menace," he said. "We are sending you to find Akori and kill him. Do not waste your time trying to take him alive; there will be no reward for that. Kill the boy, and you will be welcome in the house of the Pharaoh for ever after. Gold, riches and the favour of Set will be yours."

The favour of Set! The soldiers began to smirk at one another. This day had not gone so badly after all!

"Behold!" cried Bukhu. "Set sends you a little of his favour in advance, to help you on your mission. He has given you a gift!"

The soldiers looked around, confused. There was no sign of any gift. What did the priest mean?

Bukhu barked an order. Slaves ran to the courtyard doors and began to heave on them. From outside there came a ghastly hiss.

The gates swung open. Oba gasped in awe as he saw what was waiting out there, and the soldiers gasped with him. The hissing sound grew louder.

As the gift of Set began to enter the courtyard, Oba rubbed his hands together with glee. "Time to die, Akori," he whispered to himself. "Time to become a feast for my vultures..."

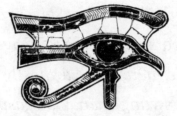

# CHAPTER ONE

Akori, Manu and Ebe jostled their way through the crowded market square. The High Priest had sent them to buy some cooking oil for the temple. It should have been a simple task but so far it was proving far more difficult than they had expected.

"Why is everyone in such a bad mood?" Manu grumbled as a servant carrying a large pot on his head shoved past.

"I don't know," Akori muttered, "but if one more person treads on my foot I'm going to cut off their sandals with my *khopesh*."

Next to him, Ebe grunted. She wasn't able to speak, but Akori could tell from the cross expression on her face that she wasn't happy either. Normally the market was a fun place to be. It was where people came to barter and trade and catch up on the latest news – but today it felt very different. Instead of laughing and chatting, people were pushing and shoving and shouting at each other to get out of the way.

Up ahead of them, a crowd had gathered around the oil merchant's stall. Akori heard something smash and then a shout.

"You broke my pot!" a man yelled.

"You tripped me!" another yelled back.

The crowd parted slightly and Akori saw that the men had started fighting.

Before long another man had joined in. And then another, until almost everyone who had been standing around the stall was rolling on the dusty ground, kicking and punching wildly.

Behind the stall, the wizened merchant began hurriedly loading his jars of oil onto his donkey. Then he dragged the donkey off down a narrow alleyway.

"I don't like this," Manu called to Akori above the din. "Something's not right."

Akori frowned. "I know. We need to get back to the Temple. Come on, Ebe, let's go."

As Akori led them back through the jostling crowd, he thought of all the terrible things that had happened to Egypt since the evil God Set had imprisoned five of the good gods. The capture of the Sun God Ra had led to a drought. When the Guide of the Dead, Anubis, had been imprisoned inside the Great Pyramid, the undead had started plaguing the living. And when the Goddess Isis had been trapped inside a watery dungeon, the River Nile had flooded. Akori had since released all three of these Gods but two more remained imprisoned – Sekhmet the Warrior Goddess, and the leader of the good Gods, Horus himself. Akori couldn't help thinking that what was happening in the market was somehow linked to this.

When they got back to the temple, they found the blind High Priest anxiously pacing inside the entrance.

"Akori, Manu, Ebe, is that you?" he asked as they came crashing through the door.

"Yes. Is everything all right?" Akori said, rushing to take hold of one of the High Priest's frail arms. He'd never seen the old man look so worried.

"Two of the trainee priests have had a fight," the High Priest said.

"What?" Manu exclaimed. "But priests never fight!"

The High Priest sighed. "I know."

"How did it happen?" Akori asked.

"I'd asked them to help each other with their study," the High Priest explained. "But then they started arguing over one of the scrolls and before I knew it, they were fighting. It was as if they'd been possessed by one of Set's demons."

"People were fighting in the market too," Akori said. "Everyone seems so—"

Akori was interrupted by the *slap-slap-slap* of sandalled feet running fast, then the storeroom door flew open with a crash. One of the High Priest's servants stood in the lamplight, panting.

"Come quickly!" he gasped. "The fire in the great hall – it's burning out of control!"

They all raced to the door of the great hall,

where they saw a strange, flickering light. Together they rushed in.

The priests had been preparing for a meal, but now overturned tables lay in disarray. The hearth was overflowing with leaping yellow flames, as if a whole barrel of oil had been hurled into it. Tongues of fire licked at the blackened ceiling.

Akori sat the High Priest down on a bench by the door. "Stay with him, Ebe," Akori said. "Make sure he doesn't get hurt."

Ebe nodded, and held the High Priest's gnarled hand tightly in hers.

"We'll be burned alive!" one young priest screamed as he ran past. "The Temple will be destroyed!"

"Don't be a fool!" shouted another. "Fetch water, quick!"

Priests came running from the kitchens, carrying basins and pots full of water. Just as the first of them was about to throw his jugful onto the roaring flames, Akori felt a searing heat on his upper arm. For a second he thought the fire had scalded him, but then he saw his birthmark burning with a bright golden light. The sign! Horus must be trying to appear to him.

"Stop!" he shouted.

The priest just stared and shook his head. He made as if to throw the water, but Manu grabbed his arm hard.

"We have to trust Akori!" he said to the furious priest.

Akori felt grateful for Manu's faith in him. It was a grave offence for a trainee like Manu to lay hands on a priest. Hoping he hadn't doomed them all to death in a fiery furnace, Akori looked into the flames. They made his eyes sting, but he refused to look away…

He'd been right! The image of Horus, tall,

muscular and hawk-headed, began to form in the midst of the flames – and then broke apart.

Akori's heart lurched. Was Horus too weak to reach him? The flames drew together a second time, and this time the image held, but only just. Horus reached out to Akori, clearly struggling. The flames formed his body, but the dark smoke of the fire shaped itself into black manacles, binding the God's wrists and feet.

"Akori!" came the noble voice, now harsh and faint. "Hear me...there is so little time!"

Akori kneeled. "My Lord, I am here." Behind him, he heard the priests kneeling and putting down their vessels of water.

"Seek...Sekhmet," Horus urged. "Set holds her prisoner. If she is not freed soon, evil will surely triumph and all your efforts will have been for nothing!"

23

"Sekhmet!" Manu whispered. "The lion-headed one!"

"Sekhmet is the Goddess who restores order," Horus said. His image shimmered unsteadily as if it were about to break apart again. "Without her influence, peace is breaking down. Chaos reigns. People fight one another for any reason...or for no reason at all."

"I understand," Akori nodded, thinking of the scenes in the market.

"Egypt needs Sekhmet to do battle against the evil Gods!" cried Horus. "She is the fiercest of all warriors! But you must be very careful – she will be guarded by—"

But his words were lost as the fire blazed up once again, and the heat became unbearable. Some tremendous force of evil was clearly trying to break the communication. Despite the heat, Akori shivered. The dark God Set had allies, fellow Gods of evil. They were the worst of all foes to face. Which one would he have to confront next?

With a tremendous effort, Horus appeared again. "...and the Minions of Set!" he gasped. "Beasts...that walk...and crawl upon the sand! Akori, I am sorry...there is not time to warn you of everything..."

Quickly, before the contact was broken again, Akori asked, "Lord, where should I seek Sekhmet?"

"She is imprisoned in the heart of the Sahara desert," came the reply. "In the Hidden Fortress of Fire! Above all else, beware—"

The furnace roared like a monstrous beast. As Horus vanished in the surging flames, Akori could just make out the words "...terrible...Goddess...winged...devour..."

Akori took a step back and shuddered. He had thought his previous battles had been difficult, but something told him this next one would be the hardest yet. Who or what were the Minions of Set – and who was the terrible Goddess Horus had been trying to warn him about?

# CHAPTER TWO

As soon as the fire had died down and order
had been restored in the great hall, the three
friends gathered by the Temple door. There
was not a moment to lose – they had to set
out on their quest into the desert straight
away. The High Priest had ordered that some
bags of food and a waterskin each be brought
to them. It gave Akori a strange feeling to
think that was all he would have to eat and
drink for the next week. There were no inns
in the desert.

As usual, Manu was lugging his bags of scrolls along with him. Nothing Akori could say would persuade the boy to leave any of them behind. Manu would just as soon have left his arms and legs behind as his scroll bags.

Ebe, as always, took nothing but the tatty slave-girl's clothes she always wore. Even her feet were bare.

The blind High Priest loaded them up with a few extra waterskins as they prepared to leave. "Take as much water as you can carry unless you want to die of thirst!" he advised.

As they turned to say their goodbyes, the High Priest laid a warning hand on Akori's shoulder. "Beware the desert, my young friends," he said. "There are deadly creatures there...scorpions, snakes, all manner of hunting beasts. Not to mention the Minions of Set!"

"What are these Minions of Set that you and Horus speak of?" said Akori.

The High Priest frowned. "Many of the unnatural things that have been unleashed from the Underworld have fled to the desert," he said gravely. "They prey upon travellers. There is nowhere to hide in the open sands, under the glare of the burning sun."

"We'll be careful," Akori promised, but he couldn't help feeling alarmed at the High Priest's words. To try and reassure himself, Akori looked in his pouch at the gifts he had been given by the Gods he had released. As well as the Scarab of Anubis, which could heal even the most deadly wounds, he carried the Talisman of Ra, filled with the sun's holy power, and the Ring of Isis, which could make the wearer invisible. And, of course, there was the gift from Horus himself, the golden *khopesh* sword that hung from Akori's belt. Horus had given it to him on the first day of his quest. That enchanted razor-edge could surely cut through anything. But would it be strong enough to free Sekhmet?

Putting his worries to the back of his mind, and bidding the High Priest farewell, Akori led Manu and Ebe out towards the desert sands. At first the warmth of the rising sun in the east was like an old friend greeting him. But as the hours of travel wore on, the desert grew hotter and hotter. By midday the heat had become unbearably harsh, and Akori suggested they stop for a water break. There was no shade, so they squatted down on some sandy rocks and passed around the bulging waterskins.

"Akori, come and look," said Manu, pointing to an image in one of his scrolls. "This is Sekhmet."

The Goddess had the body of a warrior woman and the head of a lioness. Her fierce jaws gaped, showing rows of sharp teeth. She was holding up one hand, as if to stop evil in its tracks. On the other arm she bore a shield.

Akori felt awed. "I'm glad she's on *our* side!" he said. "Look at her, Ebe!"

Ebe gave Akori a knowing grin, as if to say, *Yes, isn't she amazing?* Ebe must have seen images of Sekhmet at the Temple, Akori guessed. What an ally Sekhmet would be! But no wonder Egypt was descending into chaos with this powerful Goddess imprisoned and no longer able to keep order. As Akori thought of Sekhmet in prison, her great lioness head hanging in defeat, his awe gave way to sorrow and anger. For such a mighty Goddess to be locked up like a wild animal, caged and shamed... Set would surely answer for that, along with all his other evil deeds.

"Don't worry, I'm coming to set you free," he murmured to Sekhmet's image.

Manu unrolled another scroll. "I think we're going the right way, but I'm just going to check the map," he explained.

"How do you even make a map of a place like this?" Akori asked. "There are no landmarks! There's no anything!"

Manu pointed out across the desert. "Look at the rock formations! That one over there looks a bit like a sheep lying down, that one's like a capsized sailing boat, and that one – no, the other one, the one that looks like a man's nose – marks the way to the hidden fortress."

"So where's the fortress on the map?" Akori said.

Manu pointed silently at the map's very centre. A wind from nowhere fluttered the map's edges. As Manu began to roll up the scroll again, the world suddenly went dark.

"What the...?" Akori looked up.

Something huge passed between them and the sun, casting a vast shadow. The next moment, the sun was in his eyes and he could see nothing at all.

Akori shielded his eyes and tried to see what had flown over them, but the sun was blinding him. Whatever it had been, it was monstrous in size. Perhaps bigger than a lion.

"Did you see that?" he asked the others. "What was it?"

Manu looked around, then pointed to the sky with a yell. Something enormous was swooping back in their direction, blotting out the sun. Akori saw huge wings beating and smelled something foul and rank. A blast of wind whipped up the sand, forcing him and Ebe to their knees. It was coming! He glimpsed a gaping beak, an eye as big as a round shield. Then the massive body roared past overhead. Gritty sand blew into Akori's face. He looked up and saw the fiendish creature clearly for the first time. It was a vulture, the largest he had ever seen. It was circling above them, horribly silent for something so big. When vultures circled like that, Akori knew, they were waiting for something down below to die. And then they would come and feast.

Ebe made a terrified yowling sound in her throat.

Akori reached for his *khopesh*. "I'm not dead yet," he snarled. "You want a fight, you'll get one!"

As if it had heard him, the vulture began swooping down towards them. This time it beat its wings so hard that a huge cloud of sand filled the air. Akori cried out as it stung

his eyes. He lashed out wildly with his sword but it was no good – he couldn't see a thing. He heard a thud and then a yelp and then slowly the sand cloud began to clear.

Akori rubbed his eyes and watched as the huge shadow of the vulture sailed over the dunes away from them. He and Ebe got to their feet and dusted themselves down.

Akori felt a surge of relief. "That was too close," he gasped, turning round. "Right, Manu?"

There was no answer, and no sign of Manu.

"Manu?" he said again, feeling a sickening dread rising in his chest. He and Ebe looked around desperately. "Manu!"

Ebe tugged at his sleeve, pointing at something.

A single fallen sandal lay on the sand, half-buried where it lay.

# CHAPTER THREE

"Manu, where are you?" yelled Akori. He scrambled up a dune with Ebe close behind, hoping for a better view.

There was no sign of Manu anywhere. Empty desert stretched as far as they could see. It could mean only one thing.

"The vulture's taken him! We have to rescue him!" Akori racked his brain. "If the vulture's working for Set then it will be after me not Manu. When it realizes it's got the wrong boy it's going to be really angry – and

it will come back. I'll have to fight –
somehow I'll have to force it to bring Manu
back."

He brandished his *khopesh*, feeling its
reassuring weight in his hands. The sword
had destroyed mummies, shattered stone,
killed venomous serpents...it had even saved
his life from the ravenous Sobek, the
Crocodile God. But would it be able to help
them against this new enemy?

Ebe whined. She tugged at him again and
pointed to the horizon. A distant black shape
was winging its way towards them.

"There it is!" Akori yelled. "Get ready to
run, Ebe."

The vulture was closing in fast. Ebe's eyes
were wide with panic. Akori had told her to
run, but there was nowhere for her to run to!
Then he remembered the ring that Isis had
given him. It gave the power of invisibility!

"Ebe," he said, "hold onto my arm and don't let go!"

Ebe clung on tight. He felt her sharp nails through his sleeve. The vulture was coming in for the kill, swooping low.

"Lady Isis, Queen of Magic," Akori prayed, "help us now!" He gave the ring a twist, hoping Isis would hear him.

What happened next took him completely by surprise. His shadow vanished. One moment it was stretched out across the sand, and the next – nothing! Then Akori understood what had happened. The sun was shining right through them. Isis had heard him, and they were invisible! The vulture gave an angry croak. Confused, it sailed past above them. Another sound went by, like faint yelling, then that too was gone.

"It can't see us!" Akori whispered to Ebe.

The vulture hovered above them.

Stretching its long neck out, it hunted for its prey. It gave another croak, this time of frustration.

Akori felt a grim satisfaction. The ugly thing would go hungry tonight. But what about Manu? He had to face up to the vulture to get his friend back. Then he heard the yelling again. It was coming from the vulture's claw. Something was flailing about in the vulture's grip. Manu! Thank the Gods!

"Don't worry, Manu!" Akori called out. "I'll rescue you!"

"*Akoriiii!*" Manu screamed. "Where are you? I can't see you!"

Akori had to get the vulture's attention somehow. Maybe he could throw something – but what? His gaze fell upon his waterskin.

He hefted the waterskin and threw it as high and far as he could. The moment it left his hand, it became visible. It flipped end over

41

end and finally thumped into the sand at the foot of the dune.

The vulture cawed in triumph. It plunged out of the sky, splaying its claws wide. Manu fell, arms and legs flailing, hit the ground and went tumbling down the sandy slope. The vulture tore at the waterskin, bursting it. Its huge beak ripped the leather into ragged strips.

Manu stumbled to his feet. The fall had stunned him. He squinted around, looking for Akori. Behind him, the vulture pecked and tore. Dark blotches appeared on the sand as water gushed from the ruined waterskin.

"Run!" Akori screamed at Manu.

Manu looked around, completely confused. "Where are you hiding? Come out!"

"It's no good. We're going to have to grab

him!" Akori told Ebe. "Come on, quick!" He set off at a run across the sand, Ebe hanging onto his arm and running alongside.

The vulture took to the air again in a flurry of greasy feathers. There was nothing left of the waterskin now but scraps. Akori thought of what those claws could do to human flesh and put on an extra burst of speed.

The vulture banked around in a wide curve and came swooping down. Manu just stood there in a daze. He seemed completely unaware of what was behind him.

Akori ran. Above, the huge beak gaped and the vulture let out a furious shriek. The claws spread, ready to rip Manu apart.

Akori slammed into Manu, catching him around the waist. Manu turned invisible instantly, just as all three of them fell over in a jumble.

For a split second, great claws raked the sand. Then a cheated screech came from above. The vulture was winging back into the sky.

Akori held on tight to each of his friends. "Don't let go or it'll see you!" he hissed to Manu. "We're using the ring of invisibility."

"Oh, now I understand!" Manu said excitedly. "That's why I couldn't see you before!"

"We need to get out of here," said Akori. "When I say the word, everyone run together. Ready? Go!"

They set off at a sprint across the hot sand. An angry squawk told them the vulture was still up there, hunting.

Hand in hand, they ran until their chests burned and their feet ached. Once he thought they were safe, Akori looked back over his shoulder.

To his horror, he saw the vulture bearing down on them, with a triumphant look in its eye!

"It can see us!" he yelled. "Someone must have let go of me! Which of you was it?"

"I didn't!" Manu said. Ebe shook her head violently.

"Then something must have broken the ring's power!" Akori guessed desperately. "Or Isis herself has abandoned us!"

Manu had no answer to that.

The vulture was coming closer every second. It would not be tricked again. This time, Akori knew, those knife-like claws would draw blood.

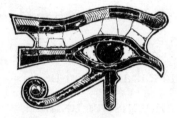

# Chapter Four

The gigantic vulture landed heavily in the sand. Its huge head lunged out, snapping wildly. Great wings buffeted Akori, sending up clouds of sand that made his eyes sting.

"It's going to kill us!" Manu howled.

"Hold on! Don't let go of me!" Akori said. The vulture was snapping here and there at random. "Look at it! It's not sure where to strike! It knows we're here somehow, but we must still be invisible."

The vulture seemed to hear him and a claw

shot out, only just missing him.

"Akori, do something!" Manu begged.
"We've got no protection! We'll be torn to
bits!"

"Use the bags!" Akori said. "Shield
yourselves with them. They're only leather
but it's better than nothing!"

Akori and Ebe backed away from the
vulture, holding their precious bags up in front
of them to ward off the claws and the vicious,
lashing beak. But Manu was moaning.

"My scrolls are in there!" he whined. "I
probably shouldn't risk them..."

Akori couldn't believe it. "Manu, you have
to—"

He never finished the sentence. The vulture
struck.

With a dreadful ripping sound, Akori felt
a claw tear into the front of his chest. A flood
of something warm and wet splashed down

his stomach. Akori knew right then he
was as good as dead. He'd been mortally
wounded. The claw had torn right through
the bag and into his body. He would bleed to
death out there and Sekhmet would lie in
prison for ever. He touched his chest and his
fingers came away wet. But it was only water,
spilling from the torn waterskin and warmed
by the desert sun, not his own blood!

The vulture began attacking again. A claw
lashed out and this time it hit home. Akori
felt Manu's whole body jerk and heard a
dreadful scream. Manu had paid dearly for
his devotion to his scrolls. He now had a
ragged cut in his shoulder, and the vulture's
claw was splashed with blood. It croaked
and the sound was like a cruel laugh.

"No!" Akori yelled. He held his last
bag up like a shield. The vulture pecked
at him, eager for the kill.

"How did that thing find us?" Akori asked Ebe angrily. "We were meant to be invisible!"

Ebe gave a groan of despair and pointed down at the sand.

Akori felt like the biggest fool in all creation. All the way they had come, three sets of tracks led across the desert. Why hadn't he thought of that?

"We were invisible, but we were leaving tracks! That's how it found us! But that means the ring *does* still work..."

Akori quickly twisted the ring off his finger and pressed it into Ebe's hand. "Look after Manu for me," he said. "I'll try to lead that thing away."

Ebe frantically shook her head and made a high-pitched yowling sound.

"I have to!" Akori insisted. "If I don't, we're all dead!"

Without waiting to argue any further, he drew his *khopesh* and broke out of Ebe's grip.

Instantly the vulture's head jerked up. It could see its prey clearly at last! Flapping up into the air, it gave chase.

Akori ran. The desert swayed and lurched around him and the air was dry and harsh in his lungs, but he ran as hard as he could. He prayed his plan was working. All too soon, he felt wind from the vulture's wings blowing cold on his sweat-soaked back. He glanced over his shoulder and saw it swooping down on him. It was now or never.

With a mighty yell he spun around, *khopesh* in hand. "Come on!" he roared. "Come and get me! Here I am!"

The vulture plunged down like the shadow of approaching death, claws spread wide for the killing blow. Akori waited, choosing his

moment, and just as the vulture struck he hacked hard at its leg.

The *khopesh* bit deep. The vulture gave a terrible, chilling scream of pain, sounding almost like a woman in agony. It flew up into the air, wrenching the *khopesh* from Akori's grip. Akori braced himself for the next attack, but the creature was flying away.

"Is that all you can take? Coward!" Within moments, the vulture was vanishing into the distance.

Akori stood, hands on hips, laughing in happy disbelief. "Minions of Set, eh? You tell your master he can expect the same from me!" He heard a weak cheer from behind him. Manu was staggering across the sand, leaning on Ebe for support. He was clutching at his wounded arm. Blood welled between his fingers.

"I think...you did it, Akori," Manu gasped.

"We're safe for now," Akori agreed. "We should rest!" He suddenly felt very tired and squatted down on his heels. "I don't think I have a drop of sweat left in me. Who's got the water?"

"Akori?" Manu asked. He didn't sound delighted any more. "Where's your sword?"

"Sword?" Without thinking, Akori groped for the blade, but there was nothing there. The leather knot hung loose. Far too late, he realized what had happened. He leaped to his feet and stared after the retreating vulture.

"My *khopesh*! It's still stuck in that thing's leg!" Akori began to run – but he knew already there was no point. He couldn't possibly catch up. There was nothing he could do. His enchanted golden sword, the gift of Horus, was lost.

# CHAPTER FIVE

Slowly, Akori trudged back to Ebe. She put his ring back into his hand.

"At least we've still got this," he said gloomily.

"And we're still alive!" Manu said, trying to smile. His brown face was ash pale now. "That's the most important thi—" He staggered forward and back, then fell over sideways like a rag doll.

Akori ran to his side. Ebe ripped off Manu's cloak.

Manu's wound was much deeper than they had realized. The vulture's claws had slashed his flesh like a butcher's knife. Blood was flowing steadily down his arm, dripping freely from his elbow and staining the sand.

Manu looked down at the gaping wound. All at once, he seemed to realize how badly hurt he was. "I spoke too soon, didn't I?" he stammered.

"Just keep still!" Akori said. "Ebe, tear off some cloth. We need to bandage this."

Beside him, Ebe began ripping long strips off the bottom of her tunic.

"You're going to be fine," said Akori, laying his hand on Manu's forehead. "Come on. It's only a scratch!"

But as Ebe laid a bandage across the wound, blood soaked through it instantly.

"Akori," whispered Manu, his voice deathly quiet. "I have to ask you something."

"Yes?"

"If I die, don't leave my body here for the vultures," Manu pleaded. "If you do…my spirit won't ever find rest."

Akori grabbed Manu's hand. "Don't talk like that! You're not going to die, not when I have the Scarab of Anubis! Why didn't I think of it before?"

Akori tore the bandage away, then quickly took the little scarab pin from the pouch at his waist and placed it on the wound. "Anubis," he prayed, "jackal-headed Lord, please help us! Heal our friend!"

The scarab twitched. Its golden wings flickered as it came to life – and then it became a blur of motion, whirring back and forth across the wound like a weaver working on a loom. Akori held his breath – the Scarab of Anubis had healed Ebe before, but she had not suffered a wound like Manu's. Would the

God's gift be powerful enough to heal such a deep cut?

Manu sucked in breath through his teeth, flinching in pain. The scarab darted here and there, moving almost too fast to see. Slowly, the patter of blood drops stopped.

"I think it's working!" Akori said. Ebe held Manu's other hand tight, looking into his face. Then, to their amazement, Manu giggled.

"It tickles!" he said, looking at his arm.

The scarab whirred its wings one last time, then fell – *plop* – into the sand, where it lay among the patches of blood. Akori carefully placed it back in his pouch. Manu's arm bore a white blotch, but no sign of any wound. Ebe shook him and made a questioning noise.

"I feel fine!" Manu said in answer. He sprang to his feet and pulled on his cloak. "Better than fine. I could walk. I could *run*!"

Ebe laughed out loud. Joyfully, they hugged each other. It was almost enough to make Akori forget about the loss of his *khopesh*. Almost.

*I've still got the other gifts, haven't I?* he told himself. *My scarab, my talisman, and my ring. Maybe I won't even need my* khopesh. But he didn't really believe it. How could he stand before Horus again without the sword? Would Horus be angry, disappointed, or even despairing? Akori dreaded ever finding out.

"Remember when Horus tried to warn you about some winged devourer?" Manu said. "I think we just met it!"

"That vulture is one of Set's beasts," Akori agreed. "I'd swear to it."

"That wasn't just a vulture," Manu said. "It was too big and too intelligent. I think it was a Goddess, and I know which one. Nekhbet."

He took a scroll from his bag and showed Akori a picture. A Goddess with a woman's body, a vulture's head and huge outstretched wings was standing by the Pharaoh.

"What's she doing with her wings?" Akori asked. "Attacking the Pharaoh?"

"No, protecting him," Manu said. "Some of the Gods will always serve a Pharaoh, even if that Pharaoh is evil. Remember the cobra Goddess, Wadjet?"

Akori remembered Wadjet all too well. She had been a huge cobra with a human face, not like this Goddess at all. "This Goddess has a human body, though," he said. "How could she be the giant vulture?"

"Sometimes the Gods can assume their animal form in order to do battle," Manu explained. "Nekhbet must be working for Oba against the good Gods. Akori, don't you understand? You faced one of the most powerful Goddesses, all on your own. And you beat her!"

Akori didn't feel like a triumphant hero though. His hand kept going to his side, feeling for the *khopesh* and finding nothing. The sword had been with him since the beginning of his quest for Horus and he was only now aware of how much he'd come to rely on it. It felt like he'd lost an arm or a leg.

"Come on. Let's get a drink," Manu said.

The three of them picked over the remains of their bags. Nekhbet's talons had torn them to pieces and the contents had been scattered. They began to find the waterskins but their joy turned quickly to despair. Manu and Ebe held up bunches of tattered rags, torn and useless. Nekhbet's sharp claws had punctured all of the skins. They continued to search, hoping they might find one intact, but not one had escaped. Every drop of the precious water had seeped away into the sand.

"What about your waterskin, Akori?" Manu said hopefully. "We still have that one...don't we?"

"Nekhbet tore it to bits," Akori replied. "I had to throw it to distract her. There wasn't anything else to throw." He swallowed hard. Already his throat was feeling dry. The sun felt hotter than ever. They were alone in the scorching desert, with the nearest water many miles away. How were they going to survive now? First the terrible thirst would come, and then the creeping madness – the curse of the desert. Every breath would be agony. In the end they would lie helpless, blinded by the relentless sun, too weary to move, praying for death... and then their bones would lie out here, unburied, scoured by the harsh desert winds.

One thought came into Akori's mind and refused to go away. At least death in Nekhbet's claws would have been quick...

# CHAPTER SIX

Akori looked ahead towards the heart of
the desert, where the baking sands were
shimmering in the heat. The dunes looked
red, like some strange, savage other world.

"We can't turn back and we can't stand
still," Akori said. "So we just keep going.
Come on." He knew he was almost certainly
leading his friends to their deaths. By the
looks on their faces, they knew it too, and
yet they stood up and followed on behind
him without a word. Akori clenched his jaw

and swore, once again, to be worthy of their loyalty.

They walked for miles through an endless oven of red dunes. Nothing stirred. There was no wind to cool them. No creatures crossed their path, not even insects. More than once, Akori wondered if the vulture had actually killed them all and they were walking through one of the many Egyptian hells. Places like this were Set's lawful dominion. Was he watching them now and laughing? Akori shook the thought out of his mind and trudged on. He longed for the cool of evening, but that was still a long way off.

The endless burning day wore away at them. The nightmare of endless thirst was unbearable. Akori's eyes ached, as if prickly ropes were being twisted inside his skull. His lips were cracking and his tongue felt like a lizard in a dry stone basin. The sand found its way into everything, clinging to arms and legs, working painfully into cracks and creases. Then the nightmare of madness began. Akori had seen nothing but blinding sun and crimson dunes for miles. Now he was seeing strange things in the corner of his eyes. Huge shapes seemed to twist and turn, but only when he was not looking directly at them, and there was a distant bell-like ringing in his ears. Akori knew they would soon start to lose their minds out in the wasteland. To keep his grip on reality, he bit his lip hard from time to time so the pain would bring him to his senses.

"Look!" Manu cried, his voice cracking. "A well! We're saved!"

Akori followed his gaze. There was something greyish-white poking out of the side of a dune. It wasn't a well – it was a dry old bush, long dead.

Manu laughed as he ran towards it. But his laughter turned to a wail of despair as he tried in vain to fetch water from the bush.

"The desert's playing tricks on you," Akori said sadly. "There's no water there."

Manu scrambled out of the dry bush and rejoined him, looking miserable. Akori looked up ahead, praying they would find some kind of shelter soon. To his amazement, he saw a majestic figure towering high above the sand, arms outstretched in blessing. Behind it, the sun blazed fiercely, like a halo.

"Horus!" Akori gasped. His prayers had been heard! Somehow, Horus had broken free of Set's prison. Had he come to bring them water? Or maybe he'd come to bring him a new sword! Summoning up his last grain of energy, Akori staggered towards the radiant figure. "Horus!" he called, his voice shrunk

to a painful whisper. "My Lord! I am here!"
He turned back to tell the others to hurry up,
but they were looking at him as if he was
crazy. Well, it didn't matter. This vision was
obviously just for him. The vast figure of
Horus towered above him. Akori flung
himself at the God's feet, grateful beyond
words for his salvation.

A terrible burning pain shot through his
arms. He yelled and pulled himself away. He
was bleeding from dozens of little scratches.
What he had thought was Horus was in fact
a massive cactus, covered in spikes. Akori
sank into the sand. He had never felt so
defeated. The cactus loomed over him, bigger
than any other cactus he had ever seen. It
seemed twisted and malformed somehow, as
if magic had warped it. Some of its spikes
were as long as his arm.

Behind him, Manu had been curiously

wandering closer. Now he suddenly screamed, "We're saved!" and ran over excitedly.

Akori tried to tell Manu that it had been an illusion, but he couldn't bring himself to say a word. He lay in the shadow of the cactus, trying to force his arms and legs to obey his will. It took intense effort, but he managed to stand up. When he saw what Manu was doing, he wondered if he had lost his mind completely! Manu had grabbed one of the long spikes and was wrenching it off. Was he trying to attack it? Then a clean, sharp smell reached his nostrils. Manu had scraped out a handful of cactus flesh and was squeezing it into his mouth. Water was trickling down his chin!

"Cacti store water inside themselves!" said Manu, digging out more wet green flesh and offering a handful to Akori. "A cactus this size? We could live off it for years!"

71

Akori sucked greedily at the pulp. Water gushed down his grateful throat, tasting sweeter than any water he had ever drunk before.

Ebe found it was easier just to rip off a big spike, stab a hole in the cactus and drink from that!

Once they had quenched their thirst and felt human again, they broke off some more cactus spikes to take with them for later, along with as much of the green flesh as they could carry.

Manu consulted his map and whistled. "We've come a long way," he said. "The hidden fortress shouldn't be more than an hour's walk from here! There's just one thing I don't understand."

"Only one?" Akori said.

"How can it be a *hidden* fortress? There's nothing here to hide it behind! Nothing but sand!"

Ebe interrupted with a whine. Then she began to gesture frantically at the ground.

"I know, Ebe," Akori said. "I'm sick of the sight of sand too."

But Ebe became even more anxious, hopping from one foot to the other and pointing downwards. Akori wished she could speak, so she could just tell him what was wrong. Perhaps the heat was muddling her head too, and she was seeing mirages like he and Manu had? She might need another drink. He offered her a wad of wet cactus, but she shooed him away.

"Manu?" Akori said. "I think Ebe's seeing something—"

But Manu was pointing to the ground too. "And so am I," he said very slowly. "Akori, tell me I'm not going mad!"

Akori looked down at the red sand.

There, staring up at him, were a pair of

cold, yellowish eyes, with slit pupils. As Akori watched, horrified, they blinked slowly.

"Look!" Manu hissed. Another pair of eyes had opened in the sand nearby. And then another.

"It's not possible!" said Akori, staring at them. "We can't all be seeing the same mirage!"

The whole world seemed to have gone insane! How could the sand have eyes? Was the desert itself coming to life?

The trio stood, gazing in disbelief at the three pairs of eyes staring back at them. Then the sand began to shift as each set of eyes rose up. Sand slid from three long, flat heads.

"Lizards!" Akori exclaimed.

# CHAPTER SEVEN

Akori watched, transfixed, as the reptiles clambered up from their hiding places.

They were huge, each one as long as a man, with red scaly bodies. Against the sand, they had been almost invisible. The camouflage was perfect!

"They might not mean us any harm," Manu said, backing away as he spoke. "Maybe they don't eat meat."

The lizards watched them coldly and began to advance. The one closest to Manu opened its mouth wide, revealing a row of teeth as jagged and sharp as broken flints, then snapped it shut.

"It doesn't look like they eat cactus, Manu!" Akori said.

Then, in one swift motion, the lizards stood up on their hind legs! They started marching down the dune, their eyes glinting with evil intent.

Akori knew then that these were not natural predators. They were supernatural beasts, Set's Minions, waiting in this dune in ambush. It all made sense now, Akori realized. Lizards were intelligent creatures. They must have known the huge cactus was the only source of water in this part of the desert. Where better to lie in wait for three thirsty travellers?

The lizards were moving in to surround the group. Akori, Manu and Ebe backed up

against each other, facing outwards.

"You don't know who I am, do you?" Akori growled at the lizards. "Because if you did, you'd know what I do to monsters!" With that, he grabbed for his *khopesh*. It was time to fight!

But he had forgotten his *khopesh* was gone. The lizards made no sound, but they narrowed their eyes. Akori knew they were laughing at him. Soon he would be within reach of those red talons. How could they fight back? They had no weapons at all! He looked over his shoulder at the other two. "We need something to fight with!" he yelled.

Ebe showed him her fists and gave a grim nod. She wasn't going to go down without a battle. As for Manu, all he had was the bag of cactus fragments. That gave Akori an idea. "Manu! Give me one of those cactus spikes!"

Manu passed Akori a long spike. Akori

gripped it like a dagger. As the first lizard
came shuffling down towards him, he jabbed
at it with an angry yell. The lizard darted to
the side and hissed at Akori as if to say, *Ha,
not fast enough!* Akori gritted his teeth and
tried again. But again the lizard was too
quick for him, slithering away though the
hot red sand. Akori wanted to fling his spike
down in frustration but he knew he couldn't
give up. He had to deal with this enemy if he
was to have any hope of saving Sekhmet.
He took a deep breath and gripped the spike,
imagining it was his golden *khopesh*. Just
thinking of his sword made his birthmark
start to tingle and Akori was filled with a
new strength. *"Aaaaarrrrrgh!"* he roared as
he charged towards the lizard. There was
a horrible ripping sound as the spike broke
through the lizard's scaly skin. Cold black
blood splashed up Akori's hand. The lizard

gave a startled hiss and pulled back. It looked wary now, surprised to have been wounded, determined not to be hurt again.

"You two, get some spikes!" Akori urged the others. "Come on! We *can* fight them!"

Manu and Ebe wasted no time in obeying. Manu held his spike two-handed above his head, waiting for a lizard to come close enough to atack. Akori felt a stab of concern for his friend. Manu was brave when he needed to be, but as a trainee priest he didn't really know how to fight. Akori prayed he would be all right.

Ebe was a different story. She gave the lizard approaching her a slow, cold grin, as if to say, *The tables have turned – better start running away.*

The lizard hesitated, looking unsure. It glanced at its wounded comrade, who was limping away from Akori, bleeding across the

sand. Seeing it was distracted, Ebe tensed –
and sprang.

Meanwhile Akori charged his own lizard
once more, letting out a battle cry and raising
the spike as if it were his lost *khopesh*. The
wounded lizard's nerve seemed to fail it
completely. It turned and pelted back across
the sand, hurling itself into the side of the
dune. It squirmed, trying to burrow down
out of sight. Akori leaped at it, and grabbed
its tail.

To his disgust, the tail fell off in his hands.
He dropped it and it lay on the hot sand,
twitching. The lizard wriggled down into the
dune, vanishing from sight.

Ebe had her lizard on the run too. It was
bleeding from a dozen scratches where Ebe
had caught it with her spike. Manu was
holding his ground, yelling bravely at his
lizard to come on and fight.

Gritting his teeth, Akori picked up the tail and started waving it at the other lizards. "Is this what you want to happen to you?" he yelled at them. As soon as the lizards saw the severed tail they froze. Then, hissing in anger, they dropped to all fours and fled away up the dune.

"Do we chase after them?" Manu panted, exhausted.

"We'd never catch them if we tried," said Akori, smiling at Manu's bravery. "But we should find out where they were going, if we can."

Manu checked his map. A look of surprise came over his face. "I could be wrong...but from the direction they went, it looks like they were making for the hidden fortress! We must be right next to it!"

Akori sniffed and looked about himself. "If we are, it must be *really* well hidden."

They all scrambled up the side of the large dune, following Manu's directions. As they reached the top, Akori gasped in amazement.

Spreading out beneath them, like a massive wound in the rocky ground, was a valley. The sloping sides were different shades of red, with clusters of dry bushes dotted here and there. They looked quite dead. All life seemed to have abandoned the place.

In the valley's very centre, carved from the same red rock that lay all around, was a squat fortress. It looked brutal and compact, like a clenched fist. The rising heat from the ground blurred the air, so the fortress seemed all but invisible against the scarlet rock.

"We've found it!" Akori cheered. "Sekhmet's imprisoned somewhere inside that thing. Come on. We have to finish our quest!"

Filled with excitement and new hope, Akori half-ran, half-slid down the side of the valley.

Then he stopped dead in his tracks. A horrendous hissing sound, like a huge kettle of water emptied over hot coals, erupted from inside the fortress.

"Wh-what was that?" Manu stammered.

"Whatever it is, it's coming this way," said Akori. "Quick!" He dived behind a thicket of dry bushes and lay low, hoping he wouldn't be seen. He beckoned to the others to join him and together they watched the fortress, holding their breath.

Nothing could have prepared them for what they saw next. Two war-chariots emerged, each one with a driver and an archer. They were wearing the Pharaoh's colours and flying his banner.

But the true horror was what pulled those

chariots: colossal scarab beetles, clambering over the sand on legs like wavering tree trunks. Foul juice dripped from their mouths and from each one came a sickening, constant hiss...

# CHAPTER EIGHT

From below came shouted orders: "Keep
a sharp watch out front! They can't be far
away!"

Horrified, Akori, Manu and Ebe looked
on as the two scarab-drawn chariots began
patrolling back and forth in front of the
fortress. The archers on the back of each one
shaded their eyes and peered out across the
desert. Both men looked strong. Akori was
sure they could fire a killing shot, even at
this range.

But death from the point of an arrow would be mercifully quick compared to what Akori imagined those monstrous scarabs would do. He fingered the tiny scarab pin in his pouch, amazed at the difference between it and the colossal hissing creatures down in the valley. Their legs left dragging marks in the sand. Each scarab must weigh as much as a hippopotamus!

Ebe looked from the patrolling chariots to Akori, her face full of fear.

"I know!" he groaned. "But I can't fight my way past them without my sword, can I?"

"What about the cactus spikes?" Manu said.

"Against creatures that size? We might as well use sewing needles!" Akori was becoming angry and frustrated. The sun on his back was burning, as if his skin was on fire. Would evening never come? Had some terrible new enemy stopped Ra's sun-barge in its tracks? The thought of Ra brought an idea into his head. "Lie low," he said to the others. "I think I've got a plan." He pulled out the Talisman of Ra. The Sun God Ra had told him it would bring him light. He could only hope there was enough light for what he had in mind – and heat to go with it!

"Ra, mighty God of the Sun," he prayed, "hear me now! Please send me your power!" Akori held the talisman up into the path of the sunlight. As the rays of the sun met the gold disc, it burned with a dazzling light. Then, as if the light was too strong to be contained, it burst out of the talisman in a brilliant beam.

Akori directed the burning ray as if he were signalling with a polished mirror. To his relief, the scarab charioteers hadn't spotted the light yet. Good! They would soon have plenty to see.

Down by the fortress's outer wall was a large clump of dry bushes. Akori angled the beam so that it pointed directly into them. He held his breath and waited. He could feel heat surging through his body, as if he were conducting the sun's power. A wisp of smoke rose up from the bushes. Akori kept the beam trained on that spot. The wisp thickened to a trail, then to a cloud. Next moment, a flickering tongue of flame was leaping up the wall. The dry bushes caught fire quickly. A dense column of smoke went wafting up. "That should do it." Akori grinned. He crouched back down beside Manu and Ebe. "Now we just have to wait for one of those thugs to notice."

He didn't have to wait long. A shout echoed out from one of the patrolling archers: "Fire! Fire!"

The archer on the other chariot drew his bow back. "Fire at what?" he demanded.

"There's a fire at the wall, you idiot!"

"Fire at the wall?" the archer yelled back, unable to believe his ears. "Have you gone mad?"

"Don't you see the smoke, you mud-eared moron? Get inside and fetch some water!"

While Ebe, Akori and Manu laid low and tried to stifle their laughter, the soldiers wheeled their scarabs around and headed back into the fortress. There was more shouting from inside, some of it sounding very angry indeed. Shortly after, the scarab-drawn chariots emerged from the fortress again. Each one was laden with clay pots, which Akori knew must contain water.

"It must be the boy Akori – the one the Pharaoh warned us about," one of the soldiers shouted to the others. "He must be hiding in the bushes. Find him and kill him!"

The drivers whacked their scarabs with sticks, sending the huge insects rearing up, then scuttling off at speed, pulling the chariots behind them. They headed alongside the wall towards the burning bushes.

"Quick!" said Akori. "It won't take long for them to realize I'm not there." He gestured to Manu and Ebe to follow him. They sprinted across the sand towards the now-unguarded fortress gate. Akori glanced up at the walls as he ran, hoping there were no more archers stationed there. The fire should have drawn them all away...but if only one soldier was suspicious enough to stay, they'd be seen. Luckily, no arrows came whizzing from the high walls and there were no shouts. Akori ducked inside the welcome shade of the gateway.

"What now?" gasped Manu.

"We keep going!" Akori said. "Look out for anything that might be a prison. We have to find Sekhmet!"

With Akori taking the lead, they ran through the long entranceway into a huge open courtyard. Walls rose up on all four sides, topped by battlements. The fortress's inner keep lay ahead, across the sandy open area. There was no sign of any guards at all.

Akori sniffed the air. He could smell burning. Was it the bushes outside? No, this was different – the smoky, bitter tang of hot metal.

He quickly found where it was coming from. Someone had set up a small brick forge in the corner of the courtyard. The embers were still burning hot, with fire irons thrust into them. Nearby lay dozens of huge curved objects, like giant thorns made from worked metal.

"Looks like nobody's here!" whispered Akori. "Good. Let's get inside that keep."

"What do you think these metal things are?" Manu said.

"I don't know, and I don't care," Akori replied. "We have to hurry!" He stepped over one of the pincer-like metal things and suddenly an image flashed into his mind. In a flash of cold fear, he understood and wished he hadn't. "Wait, Manu. I *do* know what they are."

"Well?"

"It's battle armour," Akori said, his voice filled with dread. "For giant scarabs!"

"But we only saw two."

"I know!"

Manu turned pale. "But there's enough armour here for..."

Then they heard the hissing sound again.

It was much louder this time and growing louder still.

"…for dozens of those things!" Manu finished.

But Ebe and Akori weren't looking at him any more. Ebe was pointing up at the walls, her face a wide-eyed mask of total fear.

One after another, huge black-brown shapes were swarming down from the battlements, climbing down the walls and scrambling into the courtyard. The scarabs were coming, a disgusting, bloated tide of scuttling death. The sight of their segmented underbellies and scrabbling clawed legs made Akori feel sick. They would crush and tear anything that stood in their way, and then they would gnaw at the remains. Everything would be devoured. Not even a skeleton would be left.

# CHAPTER NINE

Before he could stop himself, Akori reached for his *khopesh*. His fingers closed on nothingness. A pang of sorrow shot through him. He wondered if he could ever truly learn to live without the sword.

The scarabs bore down on the group, forcing them back against the walls.

"Let's run for the gate!" Manu yelled.

Akori knew what would happen if they did. "We'll run straight into those chariots!" he yelled back.

Then an idea came to him. "The fire irons in the forge. Quick. Grab them!"

Luckily, Ebe still had some torn strips of cloth left. Working quickly, they wrapped their hands in cloth to keep them from being burned, and seized a fire iron each.

The irons had obviously lain in the fire for some time, because the tips were red-hot and sizzling. Working up all his courage, Akori led the others back into the courtyard. The scarabs quickly scuttled towards them.

Akori jabbed at the nearest scarab. There was a ghastly hiss and an awful stench as its flesh burned. The scarab recoiled. Another, larger one surged forward, only to meet Akori's fire iron thrusting into its face. Hissing furiously, it backed away. Though its mouth twitched hungrily, dripping fluid onto the sandy floor, it kept its distance from the red-hot metal.

"Keep moving!" Akori roared, pointing out a low wooden doorway into the inner fortress. "Make for that door!"

Akori beat the advancing scarabs back, his arm aching from heat and weariness. He prayed they could be kept back for long enough. Hot irons swept in red arcs, striking sparks wherever they hit. The smell of burned insect casings became almost unbearable. Still the insects came, shoving their huge bodies forward, threatening to crush the three friends under their great weight.

The door was almost within reach. One vast, especially ugly scarab was blocking the way. Akori swatted at it with yells and curses, but it only hissed at him, no matter how much he battered it with his burning iron.

Then, to Akori's amazement, Ebe leaped forwards and smashed at it with her own fire iron. As she did so, she drew a deep breath and *hissed* back at the scarab. The noise was astonishing, like something inhuman. In a buzz of wings, the insect was gone.

Akori flung the door open and dived inside, the others following close behind. They were in a long, torchlit passageway. Manu slammed and bolted the door behind them.

With Akori leading the way, they hurried down the passage, alert for whatever new horrors might be waiting for them. It wasn't long before they reached a great hollow chamber, with a massive fire raging in its very centre. Akori couldn't see what was being burned, but he had a strange feeling that nothing was. This was an uncanny fire, fuelled by magic alone.

"We're at the heart of the fortress," he murmured. "Can't you feel it?"

His friends nodded. Leaping firelight lit up

their grimy, sunburned faces. Already, fresh sweat was beading their foreheads. Although the room was huge, the heat was intense and stifling.

"Watch out for guards," Akori warned. He could not see any, but the flickering shadows cast by the flames could hide any number of dangers. The group edged slowly around the walls, circling the great fire. On the far side, a small stone doorway stood set into the wall. The door itself was a single rough block of stone, without any handle or lever.

"There's no way to open it," Akori said.

"Wait," Manu said. "What's this?" His finger found and traced a line of hieroglyphs. "It's writing!"

Akori was excited and frustrated at the same time. He wished he were able to read it, but as a farm boy he hadn't had the education Manu had. "What does it say?" he asked.

"It's old and worn away, but I can just make it out..." Manu strained to see. "It's a riddle, I think. It says, 'Beasts must drink water, or they die. Men must drink water, or they die. But if I were to drink water, I would die. What am I?'"

From down the corridor came a horribly familiar hissing noise. They heard the scrape of huge insect legs scrabbling on stone.

"They're coming!" Manu stammered, leaping to his feet. "They must have broken through the door. We need to solve the riddle!"

Akori thought hard. He tried to imagine giving water to various creatures, imagining what would happen when they drank it. "This is stupid!" he yelled, thumping the stone door. "It's a trick! There's no living thing that dies if you give it water!"

"Maybe it isn't a living thing," Manu suggested.

"That makes no sense! How can something die if it isn't a living thing?"

Ebe whined and pointed. From beyond the flames, the sound of approaching scarabs was coming very close.

Akori looked down at his fire iron, which was no longer glowing. He could still use it as a club, but he doubted that would be enough. Perhaps he could heat it up again in the fire. He jerked his head up to look at the flames again. And then he realized – the answer to the riddle was right in front of them!

"Fire!" he said. "Fire dies if you give it water!"

The stone door slid open with a rumble. It was so small they had to crouch right down to go through it, but Akori didn't mind – at least none of the giant scarabs would be able to follow them through.

"We did it again," he laughed, hugging his friends as they slipped through the gap. "You're braver and cleverer than anyone else in the whole of Egypt."

As Manu and Ebe hugged him back something beneath their feet made a terrible grinding noise. Akori broke free from his friends' arms, only to see that the stone door was closing!

"No!" he cried, but it was too late. The stone doorway ground shut, sealing them in.

They were all alone in total and utter darkness.

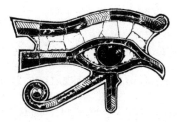

# CHAPTER TEN

For a moment, there was nothing but the dark and the sound of three frightened people breathing.

Then Akori said, as steadily as he could: "Everyone stay calm. Don't move until I say."

"Okay," said Manu's voice from somewhere nearby. "Ebe's with me. She's holding my arm. Ouch! Not so hard, Ebe!"

"All we have to do is find a wall," Akori said. "Then we can feel our way ahead."

Akori reached out in front of him with both arms, feeling for any sort of surface that he could navigate by. His fingers met nothing but empty space. He imagined the deep pits that could be just ahead, ready for him to step blindly into.

"Did you find anything?" Manu asked loudly.

"Not yet," Akori replied.

*Not yet! Not yet! Not yet!* his words echoed back at him in the darkness. That meant they had to be in a large, open chamber. All sorts of horrors could be waiting in the dark. Maybe the Talisman of Ra could light their way? Akori touched it and found it was icy cold. In his heart, Akori knew Ra could not help them again on this quest. The talisman needed to feel the sun again, far from this stronghold of evil forces, before it would regain its power. "There's nothing else for it," he said. "We're going to have to keep moving!" He reached out for his friends. "Link arms with me. If any of us starts to fall, we can pull them back up."

Together, they edged forward into the darkness. Akori felt sickly dread every time he took a step, and relief when his foot came down on hard stone instead of empty space.

They shuffled on and on.

"So far so good," Manu muttered.

But he had spoken too soon. An evil cackle sounded in their ears, echoing all around them. It sounded like an old toothless witch, laughing at some helpless victim's fate. Akori felt Ebe's grip tighten on his arm. "What was that?" he hissed.

The croaking laugh echoed through the darkness again. A breeze began to blow in his face. Then there came the *thump*, *thump*, *thump* of huge wings beating.

"Nekhbet!" Manu cried.

"Run!" Akori shouted.

Tripping, stumbling, scrambling through the dark, they ran. The sound of beating wings came closer and closer. Akori ran without thinking of what his feet might land on. He flung himself into the blackness, praying to all the good Gods that they would survive this. Then a shocking impact knocked the wind out of him.

"Ow!" he yelled.

*Ow! Ow! Ow!* his voice echoed back.

"Akori!" Manu screamed. "Are you all right?"

Akori picked himself up, wincing at the pain. He had run straight into a wall. "There's a wall here!" he called to the others. The wind from Nekhbet's wings was so strong it was ruffling his hair now. Working fast, Akori felt along the length of the wall.

"There has to be a door here somewhere!" he said through gritted teeth. "Come on, come on..." His fingers closed on a ring of cold metal. A door handle, at last! He pulled the door open and to his joy saw bright torchlight fan out into the darkness. Without looking over his shoulder he pulled the others through, slammed the door shut, and leaned against it, breathing heavily.

They were standing in a tiny cell with a low ceiling. Torches flamed from the walls. Akori looked around the room, thinking how easily he could have missed the little doorway in the dark. A row of metal bars closed off the back part of the room. It looked like a cage built to hold wild animals, but the bars were glowing blood red. This was clearly a prison meant to hold something more than mortal.

Akori's heart leaped when he saw who was

lying on the prison's floor, curled up asleep. It was a muscular woman with the golden-furred head of a lioness. Beside her lay a gleaming shield, as bright as silver in the torchlight.

"Sekhmet!" he said, in a voice of wonder. "You two, guard the door. I've got to set her free!"

He strode towards the cage, determined to free the Goddess. He would pull the bars apart with his bare hands if he had to. The heat in the room became more and more intense the closer he came. The glowing bars turned fiery orange. And then the terrible truth dawned on Akori – they were the source of the heat! How could he ever reach Sekhmet through that blazing cage?

The stink of hot metal filled the room and Sekhmet's lioness nose started to twitch. Her amber eyes blinked open and focused on

Akori. "What new torture is this?" she said, in a voice of rumbling thunder.

"I'm a friend!" Akori said. "Horus sent me. I've come to free you!"

Sekhmet was instantly up on her haunches, awake and alert. "Horus? You are his chosen? Then free me, young one!"

Akori looked around in despair. Horus had given him the *khopesh* to free the Gods with, but now it was lost he had no idea what to do!

"Hurry!" Sekhmet growled. "Why do you delay?"

"I can hear someone coming!" whispered Manu. "Whatever you've got planned, Akori, do it fast!"

But Akori had no plan. In desperation, he reached towards the cage door, thinking he could always heal his burns with the Scarab of Anubis, but the cage was just too hot to touch.

Manu let out a gasp of horror as the door flew open. Akori turned to see a terrifying figure stalk into the room.

It was a tall, skinny woman with the glassy-eyed head of a vulture. A pair of wings were folded behind her back. Bloodstained bandages were tied around one leg and from her waist hung a shining golden sword. Akori's lost *khopesh*!

"Nekhbet!" Akori said, horrified.

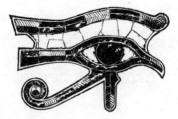

# CHAPTER ELEVEN

Nekhbet froze in the doorway. Her vulture head slowly swung around. As soon as she saw Akori, she let out an ear-piercing shriek of rage. Then she drew the *khopesh* and came lunging towards him. Akori darted to one side, narrowly avoiding being skewered by his own sword. His face was smothered with wing feathers for a second as Nekhbet went blundering past. Croaking in rage, she tried to turn around to face him again.

Akori felt a tingle of hope. Out in the

desert, the fight had all been on Nekhbet's terms. She could soar above them and dive when she chose. But in this cramped little cell, she was little better than a prisoner herself. She couldn't fight well and she certainly couldn't fly. He laughed at her. "What's the matter, beak-face? Is that leg of yours hurting?"

"Insolent *boy*!" she screeched, limping towards him, slashing wildly with the *khopesh*. Akori dodged out of the way with ease, ducking one swipe and sidestepping the next. Nekhbet's huge wings were weighing her down and at one point she nearly toppled over completely.

"Come on, Akori!" cheered Manu.

As Akori taunted the furious Goddess, Nekhbet squawked and lunged again and again, but none of her blows would connect. She was just too cumbersome.

All the while, Sekhmet watched from the cage, neither moving nor speaking. But Akori could feel her silent approval.

Nekhbet changed her grip on the *khopesh*, holding it with both hands and raising it high. Murderous hate burned in her eyes. Akori knew she was getting ready to swing the blade down like a cleaver. He looked at Ebe and gave her a quick nod. Ebe leaped through the air, landing heavily on Nekhbet's back. Her hands wrapped around the Goddess's beady vulture eyes. While Nekhbet struggled to throw Ebe off, Akori sprang at her and grabbed the *khopesh* by the hilt. Before she could react, he wrenched the sword from her grasp. At last it was his again!

Nekhbet reached up behind her, grabbed the struggling Ebe and flung the girl over her own head, slamming her down hard on the stone floor.

Ebe yelled in pain. The Vulture Goddess stabbed at her with her long beak. But the next moment Nekhbet was screaming and diving out of the way as Akori slashed at her with the *khopesh*. Now it was in his hands again, it filled him with new strength. Nekhbet tried desperately to ward off his blows, but Akori was raging and unstoppable. She ducked, and the *khopesh* smashed a chunk out of the stone wall. As Nekhbet staggered back yet again, her huge wings making her clumsy, Akori brought the sword down in a fierce two-handed stroke. Nekhbet caught the blade in her long claws and strained to keep it away from her body.

For a moment the two were locked in a trial of strength. The vulture eyes glared into Akori's, filled with black hate. Then Akori whipped the sword away and stepped back several paces. He glanced back over his shoulder. The sizzling hot cage bars were right behind him.

Nekhbet steadied herself and began a lumbering charge. She clearly meant to shove Akori against the cage and burn him alive. He would be grilled, like meat on a hot stove!

But Akori had planned for this. With perfect timing, he ran, leaped and spun around in a full circle, whirling the sword around with him for maximum force. Blade struck vulture skull with a tremendous, final *crack*, knocking her sideways.

Nekhbet staggered, clutching her head, and fell. She lay limp and unmoving, her beak open. Akori knew she was only stunned; Goddesses were impossible to kill. He might have only seconds before she recovered. "Horus," he prayed, "if you can hear me, help me now!" He turned to face the cage door and with a mighty cry, thrust the *khopesh* deep into the lock.

Akori closed his eyes, expecting to feel burning heat explode in his face. But there was no heat at all. The cage bars were dark and cold. Horus must have heard him!

The door swung open. Like a stalking lioness, Sekhmet slowly walked out of her prison. Her eyes were fixed on Nekhbet, whose own black eyes were already blinking open.

"No," the Vulture Goddess croaked, cowering away as she saw Sekhmet was free. "I had no choice! I was obeying Set!"

Sekhmet growled and Nekhbet scrambled back further. Seeing the terror in her eyes, Akori almost felt sorry for her.

"In the name of Horus the Avenger, be gone!" Sekhmet growled. "Back to the Underworld!"

And with that, Nekhbet dissolved into black smoke and seeped away into the floor.

Sekhmet turned to Akori. "Thank you, young one," she said. "You are indeed brave." She held out her silver shield. "This is my gift to you. Guard it well, and it will guard you well in return."

Akori took Sekhmet's shield from her hands.

"It will never break," she said, "and whoever bears it cannot be harmed by evil magic."

Smiling gratefully, Akori bowed down before the mighty Goddess. "I won't let you down," he said.

Akori, Manu, Ebe and Sekhmet made their way back towards the courtyard.

"I owe you my thanks too, small ones," Sekhmet said to Manu and Ebe as they walked. "Each of you has played a warrior's part today."

Manu also bowed, but Ebe just stared and stared. Akori couldn't help but smile. She was in such awe of Sekhmet. It was as if the girl had met her lifelong hero!

Akori threw open the door to the courtyard. His smile vanished. His breath caught in his throat. All he could do was stare in horror at what awaited them.

Rank upon rank of Oba's soldiers were lined up in scarab-drawn chariots, bearing the image of Set upon their shields. Dozens of spears and javelins were pointing right at Akori.

Their leader raised his sword and shouted, "When I give the word, charge! Death to the traitor!"

Akori reached for his *khopesh* and readied Sekhmet's shield. He had never faced so many, but he would fight to the last drop of his blood. Even if this was the end, he would go down fighting beside his friends, and he would take some of Oba's men down with him. He would make Horus proud.

Then Sekhmet threw back her head and roared.

The whole fortress shook. Cracks appeared in the ground. Pieces of the battlements broke off and fell with a crash. The first few ranks of soldiers went flying backwards through the air, blasted off their feet by the sheer force of the roar. Giant scarabs toppled and landed on their backs, crushing soldiers beneath them. They struggled helplessly to right themselves, but couldn't. The soldiers were thrown into a mad panic. Their scarabs were breaking loose, fleeing the courtyard in fear. It was total chaos.

Sekhmet drew a deep breath and prepared to roar again. With fearful cries, the soldiers fled, following their scarabs into the desert.

127

Within moments the courtyard was empty.

Akori, Manu and Ebe looked at each other in amazement. Akori had never seen such an incredible display of power. Slowly, they made their way out into the open desert. The sky was still a perfect blue and the sun as intense as ever.

"It's a shame those soldiers took their waterskins with them," Manu sighed. "Couldn't they have dropped one?"

Ebe offered him some cactus pulp. Manu made a face.

"Manu's right," Akori said. "Perhaps we should search this place for water. It's a long, hot journey back to the Temple."

"I think I can help with that," Sekhmet said with a smile. Her body started to shimmer and change. Next moment, a magnificent lioness stood before them.

Akori was confused. How could Sekhmet

help them find water, even in her animal form? He was not confused for long.

"Climb on my back," she rumbled, "and hold on tight! I'll have you home in no time!"

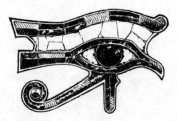

# CHAPTER TWELVE

Akori, Manu and Ebe clung onto Sekhmet's back as she raced across the valley. The fortress was soon far behind them and the huge expanse of the desert lay ahead. They moved so swiftly over the dunes it was like flying.

As the wind streamed through Akori's hair, he yelled for sheer joy, clinging tightly to Sekhmet's golden fur. She sprinted across the desert in great leaping bounds. The mounds of sand they had struggled to cross went flashing past, out of sight in seconds.

Akori had never felt so free, so alive. He felt a little sad when he finally saw the edge of the desert ahead.

They gradually slowed to a halt and Sekhmet let them dismount. The Temple stood up ahead, with the sun setting behind it. Akori was amazed. They had travelled all the way to the Hidden Fortress and back, in one day! Manu and Ebe climbed down, unsteady on their feet and thrilled from the ride. "Can we do that again?" Manu burst out, and they all laughed.

"I give you my thanks once more, Akori," said Sekhmet. "Good luck on your final quest. I fear you will need it more than ever before."

The lioness turned and began to run across the sand, moving faster and faster until she became a blur that vanished into the distance.

Ebe raised a hand in farewell, and to Akori's surprise he saw that her eyes were filled with sorrow.

The trio hurried through the Temple gateway, past priests who stared at them wide-eyed, amazed to see them return so soon. When they got to the great hall, Akori saw the High Priest anxiously pacing up and down.

"We're back!" he cried out to the old man. "We did it!"

The High Priest threw his hands up in joy and beckoned them to join him. They all sat down at one of the long wooden tables and Akori and Manu began babbling excitedly about their adventure.

"Slow down!" the High Priest pleaded. "I am an old man and my mind is enough of a muddle as it is! Akori, tell the tale a little at a time. You go at it like a starving lion devouring a meal. Manu, hold your peace until he is done."

So Akori told the story while the High Priest listened and nodded along. At the end, the High Priest reached out to feel the Shield of Sekhmet, running his fingers along its silver edge. "Once again, you have done exceptionally well," he said softly. "But remember, you still have one God left to free."

Akori gripped his *khopesh*. "I know and I'm ready!"

"You will have to be very careful, Akori," the High Priest warned. "Horus is guarded by the most evil of all the Gods, Set himself. Even though you now possess the gifts of the Gods, remember it was Set who imprisoned them. He is more powerful, more cunning and more cruel than you can possibly know."

Akori nodded slowly. It was true that he'd never faced Set directly before. The dark God had powers he couldn't even guess at. Set had overthrown many other Gods – in fact, the legends said he had even *killed* other Gods. Neither offerings nor prayers would turn his wrath aside, or so Manu had said. Set was like a violent windstorm, destroying everything in his path.

Akori looked down at his *khopesh*, glinting gold in the firelight. The High Priest was right. He knew he could count on the good Gods in his final quest. But would even that be enough?

# EPILOGUE

*The soldiers were gathered in the courtyard again. There were half as many as there had been before and the ones who remained were a sorry sight. Some limped on crutches, others kneeled in the sand to beg for Oba's mercy. A few were so swaddled in bandages they looked like unfinished mummies.*

*The war band's captain, his voice trembling, was explaining to the Pharaoh Oba where the others had gone.*

*A great many of them had run away. Some had been trampled by fleeing scarabs. Others were laid up in sickbeds, groaning. There was even a rumour going around that one soldier, awed by what he had seen, had stripped his armour off, put on a simple robe and declared himself a priest of Sekhmet, who would do only good deeds from that day onward.*

*The scarabs themselves were not in very good shape either. None of them was hissing any more. Instead they quivered, as if they too were terrified.*

*"Bukhu," Oba said to his priest, "I am confused. This does not look like a victorious army to me."*

*"Indeed, My Pharaoh," said Bukhu.*

*"It looks more like something I would scrape off my sandal."*

*"Indeed, My Pharaoh," repeated Bukhu.*

*"In fact," Oba said, his eyes blazing, "I would go so far as to say that this is a miserable, cowardly, worthless rabble."*

*"Alas, your words are filled with truth, My Pharaoh," sighed Bukhu.*

*"Do you also agree, then, that I should have my useless priest executed on the*

spot, for failing me yet again!"

"Ah, now there I must protest, My Pharaoh," Bukhu said with a sickly smile.

Oba strode up to him and began to scream and shout in his face. Bukhu patiently endured it all.

Without warning, a massive peal of thunder broke in the sky. Everyone looked up. The sky turned as dark as night. Oba fell into a fearful silence.

The dark clouds formed themselves into an image of a beast-like face. It looked like an enraged, monstrous hybrid of a donkey and a wild boar. Seeing it, the soldiers screamed and begged for mercy. Oba and Bukhu threw themselves to the ground. Set himself had come for them!

"Mortal fools!" Set roared, the sound of his voice like the fury of the storm. "You risk the loss of all I have won!"

*A fork of lightning ripped down from the sky, blackening the sand below. Oba wailed and tried to hide.*

*"Pharaoh!" boomed the voice of Set, while thunder crashed. "The pretender to your throne must be stopped, once and for all."*

*"Yes, Lord Set!" sobbed Oba.*

*"This time there can be no failure! The boy Akori must die!" The beastly head leered down. "Let him suffer the same fate as Osiris himself. Tear his body into fourteen pieces and scatter them across the length and breadth of Egypt, never to be found nor buried again. Only then will I be satisfied!"*

# DON'T MISS AKORI'S FINAL BATTLE!

## SHADOW OF THE STORM LORD

The battle to end all battles has begun. Akori must fight Set, the dark Lord of Storms himself, and beat Oba, the evil Pharaoh, to claim his rightful throne. But can Egypt's young hero finally win the crown?

TURN THE PAGE FOR A SNEAK PREVIEW!

The thing was only a few paces away. Akori had never seen anything like it, even in Manu's most ancient scrolls. It was skeletal, wearing the tattered remains of a robe, but the head where the eyes burned was like the horned skull of an antelope. Bony fingers clutched a huge wooden sickle with a sharp flint blade.

The thing gave a ghastly shriek of victory. It raised the sickle, ready to hew Akori in half. Akori backed off along the passageway, his sword trembling in his hand. The skeletal thing cocked its head, as if it were amused by this game of cat and mouse. Then it flung its jaws open and a plume of fire came roaring out.

ONE BOY... FIVE GODS... A THOUSAND MONSTERS

USBORNE

Quest of the Gods

FREE GAME CARDS

SHADOW OF THE STORM LORD

DAN HUNTER

ISBN 9781409521099

# ALSO AVAILABLE:

### ATTACK OF THE SCORPION RIDERS

For his first quest, Akori must risk his life, fighting giant scorpions and a deadly Snake Goddess. But will his terrifying battle end in victory?

ISBN 9781409521051

### CURSE OF THE DEMON DOG

The dead are stalking the living and Akori must send them back to their graves. But dog-headed Am-Heh the Hunter has sworn to destroy Akori... and no one has ever escaped his fearsome jaws.

ISBN 9781409521068

### BATTLE OF THE CROCODILE KING

Akori must brave the crocodile-infested waters of the Nile to battle two evil Gods – the terrifying Crocodile King, and his gruesome wife, the Frog Goddess – both hungry for his blood...

ISBN 9781409521075